SAM AND THE LUCKY MONEY

by **Karen Chinn**
illustrated by **Cornelius Van Wright** & **Ying-Hwa Hu**

Lee & Low Books Inc.   *New York*

MAY   2003

CH

Text copyright © 1995 by Karen Chinn
Illustrations copyright © 1995 by Cornelius Van Wright and Ying-Hwa Hu
LEE & LOW BOOKS, Inc., 95 Madison Avenue, New York, NY 10016

Printed in Hong Kong by South China Printing Co. (1988) Ltd.

Book design: Tania Garcia
Book production: Our House

The text is set in Goudy.
The illustrations are rendered in watercolors on paper. The calligraphy on the back cover represents
the Chinese characters for "Lucky Money." The illustrators added this element to the cover because Chinese reads
from right to left, and books written in Chinese open in this direction.

The editors gratefully acknowledge the Wing Luke Museum in Seattle for assistance in
transliteration of the Cantonese words and phrases used in this book.

The illustrators acknowledge, with gratitude, Peggy Lam and Ernest and Sally Heyward
for providing photo references for some of the illustrations.

10 9 8 7 6
First Edition

Library of Congress Cataloging-in-Publication Data
Chinn, Karen,
Sam and the lucky money/by Karen Chinn;
illustrated by Cornelius Van Wright and Ying-Hwa Hu.—1st ed.
p. cm.
Su[...] [...] decide how to spend the lucky money he's received for Chinese New Year.
ISBN 1-880000-53-9 (paperback)
[...]se New Year—Fiction. 2. Chinese Americans—Fiction.]
[...]ht, Cornelius Van, ill. II. Hu, Ying-Hwa, ill. III. Title.
PZ7.C4428Sam 1995
[E]- 94-11766
CIP AC

For Philip
—K.C.

With love to our mother, Liu Yung
—Y.H. & C.V.W.

Sam could hardly wait to get going. He zipped up his jacket and patted his pockets. It was time to go to Chinatown for New Year's Day!

Sam thought about sweet oranges and "lucky money": Crisp dollar bills tucked in small red envelopes called *leisees*.

Sam's grandparents gave him leisees every New Year. Each envelope was decorated with a symbol of luck: Two golden mandarins. A Chinese junk. A slithering dragon. A giant peach. Sam's leisees were embossed in gold.

Sam counted out four dollars. Boy, did he feel rich! His parents said he didn't have to buy a notebook or socks as usual. This year he could spend his lucky money *his* way.

"Sam!" his mother called. "It's time to go shopping. Hurry, so we don't miss the lion!"

"Coming!" said Sam.

The streets hummed with the thump of drums and the clang of cymbals. Everywhere dusty red smoke hung in the air left by exploding firecrackers.

"Give me your hand," said his mother. "I don't want you to get lost." Sam took her hand reluctantly. It seemed like everyone was shopping for New Year's meals. There were so many people crowded around the overflowing vegetable bins that Sam had to look out for elbows and shopping bags.

Right next to the vegetable stand were two huge red-paper mounds. Sam kicked the piles with his right foot, and then with his left foot, until he created a small blizzard. On his third kick he felt his foot land on something strange.

"Aiya!" someone cried out in pain.

Startled, he looked up to find an old man sitting against the wall. The stranger was rubbing his foot. *Bare feet in winter!* Sam thought. *Where are his shoes?*

Sam stared at the man's dirty clothes as he backed away. He found his mother picking out oranges and he tugged on her sleeve, pulling harder than he meant to.

"Hey, I need this arm," she said. "Where have you been? It's time to go."

For once, Sam was glad to follow his mother.

In the bakery window, Sam eyed a gleaming row of fresh *char siu bao*, his favorite honey-topped buns. When they opened the door, the smell of sweet egg tarts and coconut pastries erased any thought of the stranger. Sam wondered how many sweets he could buy with four dollars.

"*Nay yu mat yeh ah?*" said a young woman from behind the counter. When Sam gave her a puzzled look, she repeated the question in English. "What do you want?"

Sam was about to ask for buns when he noticed a tray full of New Year's cookies. They were shaped like fish, with fat, pleated tails that looked like little toes. He couldn't help but think about the old man again. Sam decided he wasn't hungry after all. Suddenly, he heard a noise from outside that sounded like a thousand leaves rustling. He ran to the window to see what was happening.

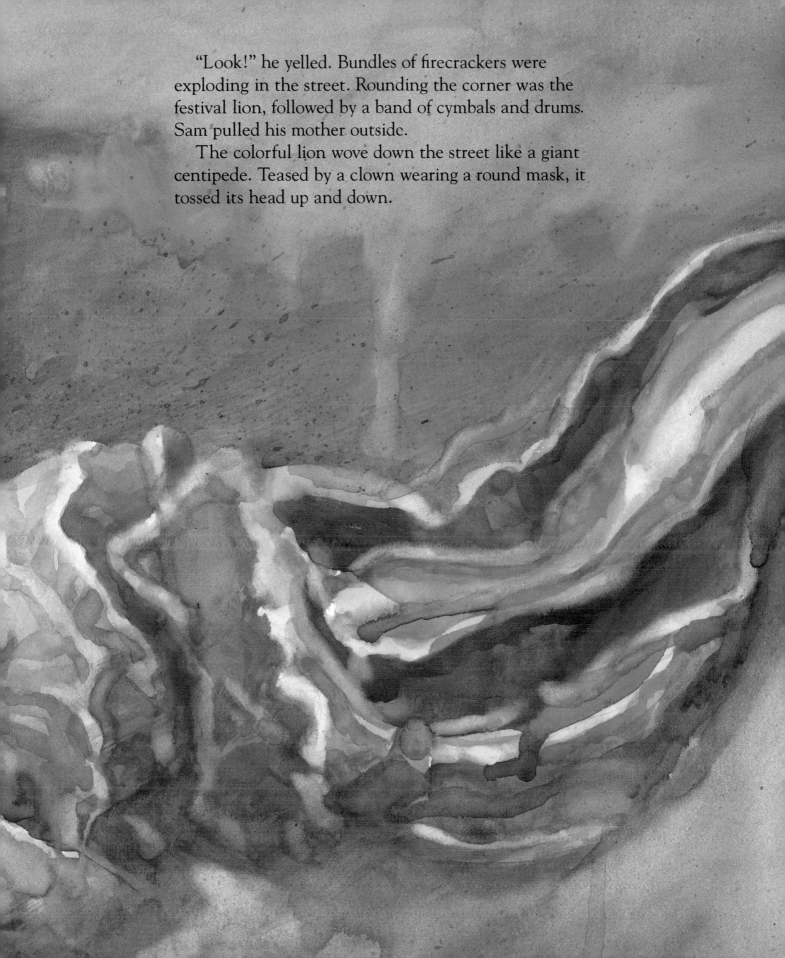

"Look!" he yelled. Bundles of firecrackers were exploding in the street. Rounding the corner was the festival lion, followed by a band of cymbals and drums. Sam pulled his mother outside.

The colorful lion wove down the street like a giant centipede. Teased by a clown wearing a round mask, it tossed its head up and down.

It came to a halt in front of a meat market, and sniffed a giant leisee that hung in the doorway, along with a bouquet of lettuce leaves. With loud fanfare, the band urged the lion toward its prize.

"Take the food! Take the money! Bring us good luck for the New Year!" Sam shouted along with the others. His heart pounded in time with the drum's beat. With a sudden lunge, the lion devoured the leisee all in an eye-blink and continued down the street. The crowd clapped and then quickly dispersed.

"That was a hungry lion," Sam's mother joked. Now he felt hungry too, and wanted to go back to the bakery.

But just then, a large "Grand Opening" sign caught Sam's eye. In the window were cars, planes, robots, and stuffed animals. A new toy store! Just the place to spend his lucky money!

Sam ran down one aisle, then another. He examined a police car with a wailing siren and flashing lights. He squeezed a talking pig and laughed at its loud "Oink, oink!" Then, he spotted the basketballs.

A new basketball was the perfect way to spend his lucky money. But when he saw the price tag, he got angry.

"I only have four dollars," he shouted. "I can't buy this." In fact, everything he touched cost more than that.

"What is four dollars good for?" he complained, stamping his feet. His mother scrunched up her eyes, the way she always did when she scolded him, and guided him out the door.

Sam couldn't help it. Even with all the shiny gold on them, the leisees seemed worthless.

"Sam, when someone gives you something, you should appreciate it," his mother said as she marched him along. Sam stuffed his leisees back in his pockets. The sun had disappeared behind some clouds, and he was starting to feel the chill. He dragged his feet along the sidewalk.

Suddenly, Sam saw a pair of bare feet, and instantly recognized them. They belonged to the old man he had seen earlier. The man also remembered him, and smiled. Sam froze in his steps, staring at the man's feet.

His mother kept walking. When she turned back to check on Sam, she noticed the old man. "Oh," she said, shifting her shopping bags so she could dig in her purse for some coins. "Sorry—I only have a quarter." The man bowed his head several times in thanks.

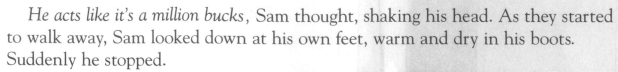

He acts like it's a million bucks, Sam thought, shaking his head. As they started to walk away, Sam looked down at his own feet, warm and dry in his boots. Suddenly he stopped.

"Can I really do anything I want with my lucky money?" he asked.

"Yes, of course," his mother answered.

Sam pulled his leisees from his pockets. The golden dragon looked shinier than ever. He ran back and thrust his lucky money into the surprised man's hands.

"You can't buy shoes with this," he told the man, "but I know you can buy some socks." The stranger laughed, and so did Sam's mother.

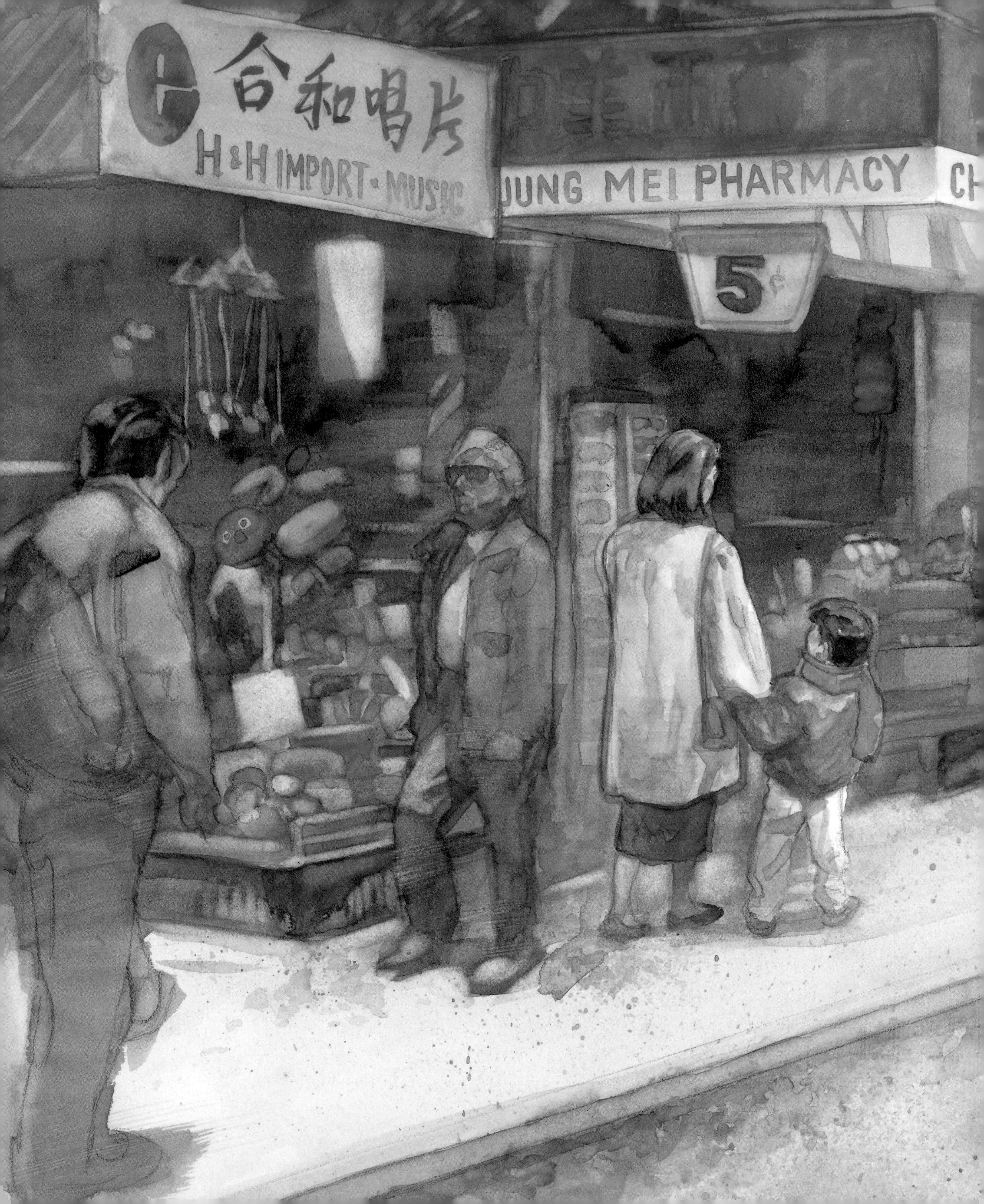
合和唱片
H&H IMPORT • MUSIC
JUNG MEI PHARMACY
5¢

Sam walked back to his mother and took her warm hand. She smiled and gave a gentle squeeze. And as they headed home for more New Year's celebration, Sam knew he was the lucky one.